# Meet the Gang

## Stuffy

Stuffy is a rambunctious stuffed dragon. He is brave and silly, with a tendency to run into things. His greatest wish is to be able to fly, like a real dragon! Whether Stuffy is trying to fly or is getting into trouble, he's always good for a laugh!

## Doc McStuffins

Doc is six years old, and she has a secret. She has a magic stethoscope that can bring her toys to life! Doc loves helping her friends when they aren't feeling their best. She makes sure to write down each diagnosis in her Big Book of Boo-Boos.

## Hallie

Hallie is Doc's lovable hippo receptionist. She keeps things running smoothly. Hallie is always ready to give Doc a helping hand, but that doesn't mean she doesn't know how to have fun!

## Lambie

Lambie is Doc's stuffed lamb who just loves to cuddle! She doesn't like to get dirty and always tries to look her best. Lambie is a loyal friend and always reminds Doc that she can do anything she sets her mind to!

## Chilly

Chilly is a hypochondriac stuffed snowman. He's always saying, "I hope I don't melt!" And when Doc reminds him that he's not a real snowman, Chilly fills with relief. He's a little stuffed snowman with a big personality.

Published by Disney Press, an imprint of Disney Book Group. No part of this book may be reproduced or transmitted in any form or by any means, electronic or mechanical, including photocopying, recording, or by any information storage and retrieval system, without written permission from the publisher.

For information address Disney Press, 1101 Flower Street, Glendale, California 91201.

ISBN 978-1-4847-0292-5
T425-2382-5-13338
Printed in China
First Edition
1 3 5 7 9 10 8 6 4 2

For more Disney Press fun, visit www.disneybooks.com
This book was printed on paper created from a sustainable source

# Run-Down Racecar

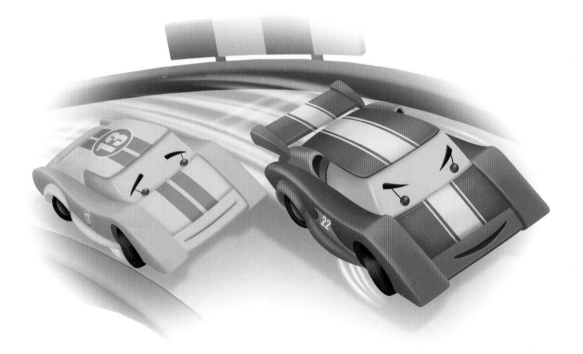

By Sheila Sweeny Higginson
Based on the episode written by Kent Redeker
Illustrated by Alan Batson

**Disney PRESS**

New York • Los Angeles

**D**oc and Donny are getting ready to race.
Donny puts Ricardo Racecar at the starting line.
Doc picks up a yellow racecar and puts it next to Ricardo.

"After Ricardo beats your car, he's going to be ready for the **Championship-Best-Racecar-Ever** race!" Donny says.

"Let's get this race going," Doc says to her brother with a smile.
The racers start their engines . . . **and they're off!**

Ricardo takes the lead.
Donny and Doc watch as the cars **zoom** around the track.
"Only one more lap to go before Ricardo wins the race!"
Donny cheers.

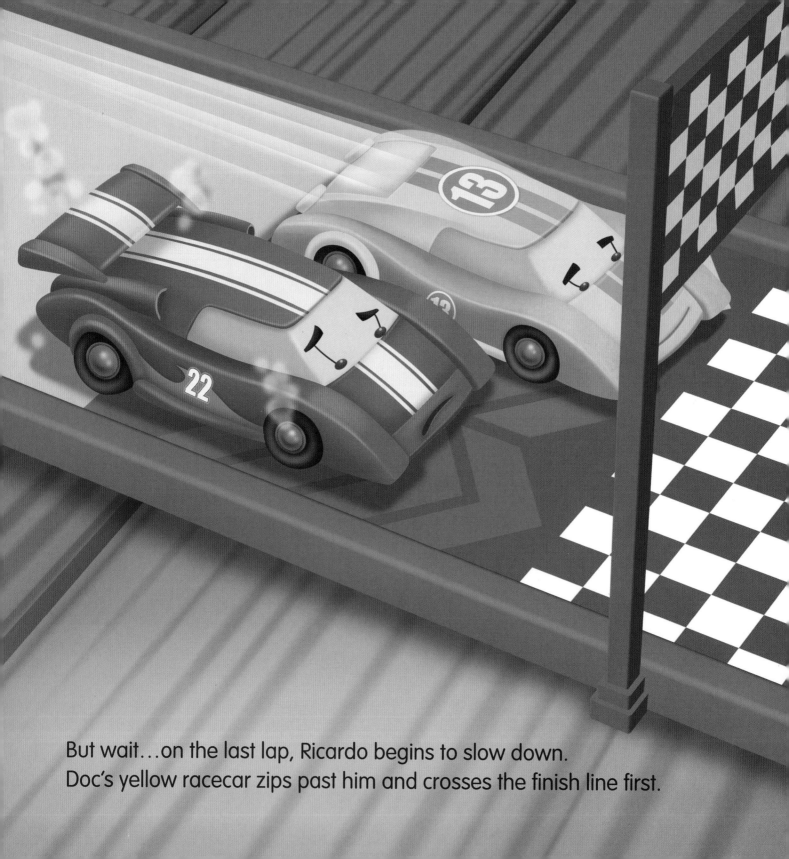

But wait…on the last lap, Ricardo begins to slow down.
Doc's yellow racecar zips past him and crosses the finish line first.

"You won!" Donny yells. "That's not possible!"
Donny's eyes fill with tears. He throws the remote control to the floor.
"I'm sorry, Donny," says Doc.

Dad comes in to see what's wrong.
"Donny, I think you need a nap," Dad says.
"But I'm not tired," Donny says. Then he yawns.

"Why don't I see if I can fix Ricardo?" Doc says.
"Good idea, Doc," says Dad.

Dad steers Donny to his bedroom.
"If you get some sleep now, it will recharge your batteries,"
Dad says.

"I'll fix Ricardo before your friend Luca gets here for the big race," Doc adds.

Doc carries Ricardo to her clinic while Donny naps.
Her stethoscope begins to glow.
Then, magically, all the toys come to life.

Stuffy sees what Doc has in her hand.
"Ricardo Racecar?" says Stuffy. "I'm his number-one fan!"

Ricardo wonders why he is being carried.
He's the greatest racecar there is.
Surely he can race his way across a backyard!

"You haven't been going as fast as usual," Doc explains.
"I'm worried something might be wrong with you."

Ricardo doesn't know what Doc is talking about.
He is faster than any racecar around!
But when Doc puts him on the ground,
he sputters and stops.

"But I have a big race today," Ricardo moans.
"Donny's counting on me!"

It's time for Doc to give Ricardo a checkup.
She lifts his hood and looks at his engine.
Everything looks okay in there.

"Can you give me a big ***vroom vroom***?" Doc asks.
Ricardo tries, but his *vroom* doesn't have a lot of power behind it.

Hallie thinks Ricardo looks worn out.

"You raced a bajillion times last night, right?" Doc asks.

"Yes, this is true," says Ricardo. "A bajillion times exactly."

Doc knows what is wrong.
"My diagnosis is **No-*Vroom-Vroom*-atosis!**"
she tells Ricardo.
Ricardo needs to recharge his battery!

Doc asks Dad to plug Ricardo into the charger.
Before long, Ricardo's battery light turns green.
By the time Donny's nap is over, Ricardo will be **all revved up**.

Later on, Donny's friend Luca comes over to play.
Donny puts Ricardo Racecar at the starting line.
Luca picks up his car and puts it next to Ricardo.
The racers start their engines . . . **and they're off**!

On the last lap, Ricardo begins to speed up.
**"Go, Ricardo! Go!"** Doc cheers.
He zips past Luca's car and crosses the finish line. Ricardo wins!
"Thanks, Doc!" says Donny. "You're the best big sister in the whole wide world!"

# Doc's Tips for Recharging Your Batteries

- Your body needs time to rest so you can have energy to play.

- Go to bed early.

- Take naps if you're feeling tired during the day.

- After you run and play, get plenty of rest.